WITHDRAWN

BY SCARLET VARLOW    ILLUSTRATED BY MARILISA COTRONEO

# CREATURE FEATURE

# The Creature in the FIREPLACE

Calico
An Imprint of Magic Wagon
abdobooks.com

FOR LILY AND JUDE, MY FAVORITE LITTLE MONSTERS. —SV

WITH ALL MY LOVE TO MY FAMILY AND MY WORK. —MC

abdobooks.com

Published by Magic Wagon, a division of ABDO, PO Box 398166, Minneapolis, Minnesota 55439. Copyright © 2020 by Abdo Consulting Group, Inc. International copyrights reserved in all countries. No part of this book may be reproduced in any form without written permission from the publisher. Calico™ is a trademark and logo of Magic Wagon.

Printed in the United States of America, North Mankato, Minnesota.
052019
092019

THIS BOOK CONTAINS
RECYCLED MATERIALS

Written by Scarlet Varlow
Illustrated by Marilisa Cotroneo
Edited by Bridget O'Brien
Art Directed by Candice Keimig

Library of Congress Control Number: 2018964981

Publisher's Cataloging-in-Publication Data

Names: Varlow, Scarlet, author. | Cotroneo, Marilisa, illustrator.
Title: The creature in the fireplace / by Scarlet Varlow; illustrated by Marilisa Cotroneo.
Description: Minneapolis, Minnesota : Magic Wagon, 2020. | Series: Creature feature
Summary: When a gremlin like creature starts wreaking havoc and getting them in trouble, brothers Jason and Elliot have to work together to build a trap and prove their innocence.
Identifiers: ISBN 9781532134975 (lib. bdg.) | ISBN 9781532135576 (ebook) | ISBN 9781532135873 (Read-to-Me ebook)
Subjects: LCSH: Monsters--Juvenile fiction. | Brothers--Juvenile fiction. | Mistaken identity--Juvenile fiction. | Trapping--Juvenile fiction.
Classification: DDC [Fic]--dc23

JFIC
VARL

5/20 RF

# TABLE OF CONTENTS

# #1
# HOME
# SWEET
# HOME

*The new house was so much larger than necessary—it almost felt wasteful,* Jason thought. He stepped through the front door beside his twin brother Elliot.

There had to be at least six bedrooms in the two-story mansion of a place. But he and Elliot would share a room, and the only other person living with them was Dad.

Jason frowned as he remembered hugging his mom goodbye earlier that morning as she cried at the airport.

"I'll be seeing you every other Christmas," she'd promised through her tears, her suitcases gathered at her feet. "And every summer you boys will fly up and stay with me for a few months."

Jason had asked her for what felt like the hundredth time why they couldn't all live together like before. But Mom answered how she always

did. By reminding him gently that they'd sold their house and that they were going to have to live separately because of the divorce.

Divorce. Jason hated the word.

"Are you kidding me right now?" Elliot said as he took a few steps into the new house. It had a spiral staircase and wooden beams that cut across the high ceiling.

"This looks like a haunted house if I've ever seen one. Are those cobwebs? How long has it been since anyone has lived here?"

The amount of space *was* surprising.

And, to be honest, if Mom were with them, Jason thought that maybe they'd have reacted to the mansion differently. They'd beg for their scooters to be unpacked so they could whiz around and have races through the hallways.

But Mom wasn't here. Instead he and Elliot just gaped at the enormous, cold space that was their new home. Their mouths hung open in the same way.

"I know it's a little rough," Dad said. He came in with two suitcases in each hand and a cardboard box tucked beneath one arm.

"I inherited it from my uncle probably fifteen years ago, and planned on fixing it up when I had time, but . . ." His voice trailed off, and he shrugged. "I never did. I didn't have time, until now."

An awkward and familiar silence fell between them. A silence that Jason was starting to recognize as a sign they were thinking about Mom.

Elliot looked at the floor and kicked at a dust bunny. Dad set the stuff down against the wall and went back out to the car to unload more boxes.

"Which room should we pick?" Jason asked his brother, who wouldn't look him in the eyes.

"I don't know," Elliot said with a shrug, and turned to follow Dad out and help. "I don't really care."

Jason stayed behind as Elliot stepped outside, now alone in the too-big house that was covered in

dust and spiderwebs. He realized with complete dismay that he couldn't remember feeling sadder than he did in that moment.

The divorce had changed everything and everyone. Mom and

Dad were always moping, and even Elliot was talking to Jason far less than he used to. What was there to look forward to?

Dad and Elliot reappeared, each of them carrying more stuff from the truck.

"We were just discussing dinner," Dad said to Jason. Elliot dropped the boxes with a loud *thunk* on the floor. "Hey, Elliot, you need to be careful with those. Some of it is pretty fragile stuff. We wouldn't want to break anything."

"No." Elliot's voice was low and flat. "We sure wouldn't want *that*."

"Watch your tone, mister," Dad said, but Elliot was already on his way back out the door.

After he took a deep breath, Dad turned to Jason. "Anyway, what do you think we should eat? Pizza? Cheeseburgers?"

More than anything, Jason just wanted to see Dad smile again. "How about Chinese?" he asked, knowing it was his dad's favorite.

"Lo mein and fried rice and sticky chicken?"

Sure enough, the corners of Dad's mouth turned up just the slightest. "That sounds great," he said, giving Jason's shoulder a squeeze before going back to work.

Jason gave one last look around the new house before going out to help.

In the far corner of the living room, which he could see perfectly from where he was standing, was a large fireplace. It was surrounded

14

by stone with an elaborately carved mantelpiece.

As Jason watched, dirt and soot rained down from the inside. As if there was something in the chimney moving around.

*A rat,* he thought as his chest fluttered in surprise. *It's probably just a rat.*

# #2
# TOO MUCH BICKERING

"Maybe we should have separate rooms," Elliot said. He stood in the doorway of the bedroom Jason had chosen. His arms were crossed over his stomach. "I mean, why not, right? There are more than enough rooms for it."

"Dad said he was going to use up the spare bedrooms," Jason said defensively. He and Elliot had always shared a room. Was his twin mad at him or something?

"Well, he said that he had ideas for *two* of them," Elliot corrected. "He's going to make one into a reading room, and one into a game room. That still leaves two rooms."

Jason blinked. Elliot was really serious! It almost felt like a betrayal of some kind.

"Did I do something wrong?" Jason asked before he could stop himself. "Why do you want to suddenly live in different rooms?"

"Not everything is about you," Elliot snapped with a surprising amount of anger. "Can you let me breathe? You haven't gotten off my back ever since we found out we were moving!"

Jason blushed, suddenly feeling embarrassed. He and his brother never fought, ever.

Mom and Dad had called them the Angel Twins, because they never went through any especially naughty phases. And they were always so serious and calm about things.

Instead of acting out, the boys had just talked to each other. Until now, anyway.

Now, they were fighting in this

enormous house that was going to take Dad months or years to fix up.

Plus, it was so cold and dark inside. Despite the high ceilings, there weren't many windows.

Between that and the webs and dust and weird creaking sounds (what had been scuffling around inside the fireplace?), Jason wished he could run away.

"What's going on in here?" Dad appeared behind Elliot. His face was red and sweaty from all the work he was doing.

"I thought I heard something from down the hall, and it sounded an awful lot like you two were arguing again. Will you ever stop? Give me and yourselves a break!"

Yet another new thing that had come as a result of the divorce. Dad lost his patience far more often and easily than he ever did before.

Between him and Elliot, Jason felt like he was walking around a dark room filled with traps, like in that adventure dungeon video game he'd been playing lately.

"Sorry, Dad," Jason and Elliot said simultaneously, in the same sort of ashamed voice.

"I don't want to hear it anymore," Dad said shrilly. He turned and left them to return to whatever he'd been doing. "There's too much bickering going on around here!"

When he was gone, Elliot faced Jason once again. "So, um. Yeah. I think I'm gonna sleep in the next one over."

Then, he was gone. Jason felt like he'd been punched in the stomach.

He walked slowly around his new room, taking in the space, wondering how he'd possibly be able to fill it enough.

The things from his last bedroom would hardly add a dent. He'd have to slowly collect things to make it feel more cozy: a rug, a desk, maybe a trunk for the end of the bed.

Jason set his hand on the wall, which was covered in peeling wallpaper and cracked paint.

Something moved on the other side of the wall.

Jason quickly pulled his hand away with a gasp. A few seconds passed, and he slowly raised his hand up to the wall again. Holding his breath, Jason pressed his palm against the cool, flat surface.

Something scurried around inside the wall, flopping around like a trapped animal of some sort.

"What in the world?" Jason said. Without thinking, he knocked on the wall.

Whatever was inside knocked back, in the same way that he had.

Jason stepped away from the wall, his heart pounding in his chest. "Who's there?" he asked. After a few moments of complete silence, he started to feel quite silly.

Was it possible that the knock was just a coincidence? A big fat rat on a loose beam that was bumping against the wall in Jason's room?

He remembered the soot falling like black snow from inside the fireplace downstairs. He shuddered.

25

# #3
# NOT A RAT

The next day, Dad went to the hardware store and Elliot closed himself up in his new room. Jason explored the house, knocking on random walls as he tried to find what had knocked back before.

No matter how many times he tried, Jason couldn't get it to happen again. He continued to wonder if perhaps he'd imagined it after all.

The last room he went into was the living room on the ground floor. The fireplace that he'd seen when he first arrived was there, like a big yawning mouth with teeth of bricks and firewood.

Jason looked around the room. He wondered how in the world Dad would ever be able to catch up with the things that needed fixing.

It seemed like far too hopeless of a chore, never-ending, all the things that needed to be cleaned or painted or nailed or replaced.

If he were Dad, he'd probably curl up under the covers and never come out.

A strange tapping noise came suddenly, from across the room. Jason realized that it was coming from inside the fireplace.

He took a few hesitant steps forward, noticing again puffs of black and gray soot falling over the wood inside.

*Scratch, scratch, scraaaaatch!* Something was crawling down the chimney.

"Hello?" Jason said.

At the same time a long-fingered hand, green and the size of a dinner plate, curled up and around the mantel from inside the fireplace. Its claws clicked against the stone.

Jason screamed and backed into the wall. As he watched, another hand appeared. It was followed by a pair of spindly arms and a hairless, little green head.

The monster crawled out from its hiding place. Its hands were exceptionally large compared to the

rest of its body. It looked at Jason and let out a deep, throaty screech.

Jason screamed louder than he ever remembered screaming. Even louder than the time he went on the roller coaster that held the world record for the longest drop.

The monster snarled but stayed on the wall above the fireplace like an oversized green spider. Its eyes were black and shining and wild.

Suddenly, there came footsteps rushing downstairs. Elliot! Elliot had heard Jason and was coming to see what happened.

But before Jason's brother entered the living room, the monster with the long-fingered hands scuttled back into the fireplace. It crawled into the chimney and disappeared once again.

"What's wrong?" Elliot cried as he burst into the room. "You sounded like you were being kidnapped by a werewolf!"

Jason could still feel his knees shaking. He didn't tear his eyes away from the fireplace, fearing that the thing would return.

That must have been what he felt in the wall upstairs. Now that he thought about it, Jason realized that his room was directly above the living room . . . and the fireplace.

"There was a monster," Jason

whispered, and Elliot let out a sound of frustration.

"Are you for real, Jason?" he nearly yelled. "I thought something was seriously wrong with you when I heard you scream. I almost had a heart attack! I don't really know why you thought that it would be funny, but it isn't, it *wasn't . . .*"

"I'm not making it up," Jason urged, turning away from the fireplace at last. "Elliot, I promise. It had huge creepy hands and claws and its skin was green!"

Elliot stared at his twin as if trying to figure out the answer to a confusing puzzle. He crossed his arms over his chest.

"Look, is this about us living in separate bedrooms? I told you—"

"No." Jason was near tears. "I promise this has nothing to do with that! I noticed something in the fireplace on the first day here and I didn't think anything of it. But then I heard it behind the wall in my room. The chimney must run up against my wall!"

"Stop it!" Elliot stomped his foot, making Jason jump. He could see the fury on his brother's face. "Stop lying to me! You're supposed to be my best friend, but lately you've completely changed."

"*I've* changed?" Jason said, and let out a humorless laugh. "Okay."

Before either of them could say another word, the monster's deep shrieking growl rang out from the fireplace. Soot began to snow down again.

# #4
# IN PIECES

"What in the—" Elliot said, at the same time Jason yelped, "I told you!"

The monster crawled out faster than it had before, quickly scurrying up the wall to the ceiling. Only then did it turn around and let out another roar at the brothers.

It lifted an enormous hand to point a long, clawed finger as it bared its small but pointed teeth.

Jason backed up, eventually bumping into Elliot, who grabbed him and squeezed his arms to keep him still.

"Don't move," whispered Elliot as the green creature quieted and started moving down the wall. "Don't make any sudden noises. We don't want to scare it and make it attack us."

"I think it wants to attack us anyway," Jason answered quietly. He didn't blink as he looked at the ugly clawed thing in terror.

The creature jumped to the floor and crawled over the hardwood. The boys screamed as it leaped to the opposite wall and knocked down an enormous antique mirror that Dad had only mounted yesterday.

The mirror fell from the wall and shattered. Shards of glass exploded across the floor, sliding over the wood in hundreds of pieces.

Both boys stood frozen in shock. The monster scuttled back to the fireplace, crawling inside and disappearing once again.

At the same moment, the front door opened. Dad stepped into the house, struggling to carry the supplies from the hardware store.

He kicked the door closed behind him and noticed the boys standing there. He started to smile before his eyes fell on the mess of glass covering the floor.

"What did you two do?" he asked, dropping everything to hurry over. "Step carefully, for goodness' sake, there's glass everywhere!"

He spotted the antique mirror's busted frame on the ground, and his face fell even further. "Oh, boys . . . that mirror was so expensive! How could you do this?"

Elliot and Jason started talking at the same time. "We didn't do it!" Jason swore, as Elliot cried out, "It was a monster!"

Once Dad had led them safely away from the glass, he got a broom and started sweeping up the shards. They clinked as they were gathered into a pile.

"I can do that, Dad," Jason said, reaching for the broom. "You don't need to—"

"You've done enough," Dad interrupted. "I'd like for you and

your brother to please go upstairs, to your rooms. We'll talk about this once I've cleaned up the mess."

"Dad," Elliot said. "I know it sounds crazy, but I promise, there really was a monster. It lives in the fireplace! Please, just take our word for it. We wouldn't lie about something like this."

Dad shook his head as Elliot spoke, as if getting angrier with every word.

"Stop. You're not fooling anybody by sticking to the monster story. I

can't believe that either of you could ever think that it was a good idea to make up a *monster* as a cover story! You're way too old for this."

Jason started to argue. But Elliot shot his brother a look that made him go quiet.

He knew what his twin was thinking. Trying to convince Dad that the monster was real was a lost cause—it'd only make everything worse.

They were going to have to figure out a way to deal with the creature

on their own. Prove its existence to Dad somehow when it wasn't hiding deep in the chimney.

The boys walked upstairs to their bedrooms, their heads down as Dad muttered and cursed under his breath.

"What are we going to do?" Jason asked when he reached his room, but Elliot kept walking. "Elliot?"

"I don't know," Elliot said. He lingered in his own doorway. "As usual, Dad's more focused on his own problems than ours."

46

"A monster is everybody's problem," Jason answered with a frown.

But Elliot was already out of sight, closing the door to his room and leaving his brother alone once more.

# #5 UP IN SMOKE

Punishment for breaking the mirror was that Elliot and Jason had to help Dad work on the house the next day. They cleaned and carried things back and forth and whatever else was asked of them.

Jason secretly hoped that the creature would come out now that Dad was home. If he saw the thing with his own eyes, then he'd know

they'd been telling the truth about the mirror.

But of course, the creature in the fireplace stayed put, no matter how many times Jason went into the living room and made noise in an attempt to provoke it.

They ate a late lunch in the afternoon. Both boys were unable to sit still at the table. Jason realized that Elliot kept glancing at the doorway leading into the dining room, as if expecting to see the monster.

"How are your insect projects coming along?" Dad asked casually as he chewed his sandwich. "They're due tomorrow, aren't they?"

Jason and Elliot looked at each other in panic. Jason could tell that his brother had forgotten about the school project just as much as he had. Neither of them had even gotten started!

"Yeah," Elliot said, lowering his eyes to his plate. "They're both going pretty well so far. Just gotta finish them up tonight."

Jason breathed a sigh of relief. Elliot was the quick thinker of the two, and Jason was grateful for it.

"Good job," Dad said, then stood to clear his plate. "I guess you should go do that, then, when you're finished with your lunch."

"Okay, Dad," Jason said, and Elliot nodded. As soon as Dad was gone, Elliot turned to look at Jason with wide eyes.

"There's still time to do them well enough to get a good grade," Elliot said. "We just have to focus."

"Can we talk about the creature first?" Jason couldn't understand how Elliot was able to stress about homework after what they'd seen.

"I don't think I'll be able to concentrate on anything until we've figured something out. How are we supposed to sleep knowing that . . . *thing* . . . is in the chimney?"

"Yeah," Elliot muttered, leaning back into his chair. "You're right. I've been nervous since it happened. If it broke the mirror, what else will it do?"

Both boys shuddered.

"But how can we trick it into coming out when Dad is home?" Jason asked. "I already tried that earlier today. It didn't work."

"What if," Elliot said, his eyes shining. "We didn't have to trick it into coming out?"

"What do you mean?" Jason furrowed his eyebrows together.

"It's in the fireplace." Elliot stood up, motioning for Jason to follow him. "What if we just lit a fire?"

Of course! Jason followed his

brother, rubbing his hands together nervously. They could smoke the creature out of the chimney, force it to flee the house forever.

At the very least, they could feel safe when the fire was lit. The creature may have been scary. But there was no way it'd be able to crawl through fire without getting hurt.

Elliot called Dad into the room and asked him to light a fire. "We want to work on our projects in here," he said. "But it's so cold!"

Dad, in a hurry to go back to what he was doing, agreed all too easily.

Once the fire was lit, the boys listened for screeches or roars from the chimney, but there came none. Perhaps the creature had left.

For the first time in hours, Jason could breathe a sigh of relief. No more worrying about that creature!

The boys were in great spirits as they completed their projects, sitting on the rug before the fire. Jason's chosen insect was the grasshopper; Elliot's was the stag beetle.

Each boy created a big poster listing various information about their insect's eating and living habits. They also built cardboard replicas and painted them. By the time they finished, it was bedtime.

Elliot made Dad promise to keep the fire going for as long as he could.

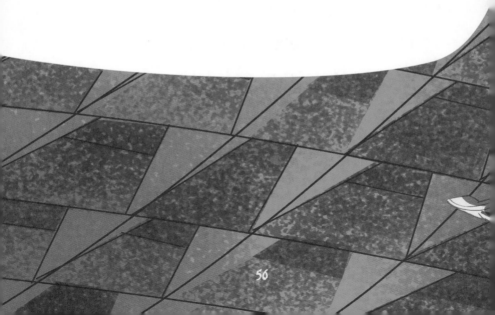

# #6
# BUGS, BUGS, BUGS

The next morning was Monday, and Jason woke up early.

The new house was a half hour away from their old home. Jason and Elliot were able to attend the same school. Jason was grateful for that, even if it was no longer Mom getting them ready for their day.

It was only the third day without seeing her. He missed her so much

already. He'd have to call her as soon as he got home from school.

Jason got dressed, brushed his teeth and hair, then went down to join Elliot and Dad in the dining room for breakfast.

When it was time to leave, the boys ran into the living room to collect their projects. The poster boards were still nice and rolled up like they'd left them, the paint on the cardboard replicas finally dry.

Before leaving the room, Jason gave a last look at the fireplace.

Soot fell from inside the chimney again. His heart skipped a beat.

"The creature isn't gone," Jason told Elliot once Dad had dropped them off. They were heading into school together. "I just know it."

"Relax," Elliot said after Jason mentioned the soot. "That doesn't mean anything. It could have been a strong breeze coming in through the top of the chimney or something. Let's not jump to conclusions."

But Jason felt a seed of dread bloom in his stomach. When it was

time for the insect presentations, Mrs. Blackwood asked the students to set up their insects on the counters along the edge of the room.

Jason and Elliot started setting up beside each other. Jason was relieved that Elliot didn't make a point to set up far away from him. Maybe they were still best friends after all.

When the teacher came to grade the boys' projects, she inspected their poster boards with an impressed smile. "Great information included

here," she said. "Let's see your replicas, now!"

Mrs. Blackwood picked up Jason's grasshopper in her left hand, and Elliot's stag beetle in her right. There came a strange scratching sound from their projects, as if there was something inside.

Jason was confused; they hadn't put anything inside the replicas when they made them last night.

"Excellent craftsmanship, boys," the teacher said. "Jason, I especially love the details you painted on the

62

wings, and Elliot, great shape with these horns."

Suddenly, a dark shape appeared on the teacher's hand. Jason gasped when he saw that it was a beetle. Before she could react, another shape appeared on her other hand: a dark green grasshopper.

Mrs. Blackwood let out a startled sound and dropped both cardboard insect replicas.

When they landed at her feet, they each broke open at the heads. From the openings in the

cardboard poured forth a swarm of scurrying black beetles and frantic, jumping grasshoppers.

"What in the world?" Mrs. Blackwood cried. The kids nearby screamed and stepped back from

the insects that were crawling and jumping. "Jason and Elliot, what is the meaning of this?"

The twins stood in shock, staring at the insects with their mouths hanging open. How had all those grasshoppers gotten inside Jason's cardboard replica? And how had the beetles gotten inside Elliot's?

Jason could feel his face warm as he figured out the answer: the creature. The creature had done this somehow, to get them in trouble, just like with the mirror!

Jason and Elliot were sent to the principal's office. Mrs. Blackwood called Dad to tell him about the incident. It was the first time either of the boys had gotten into any sort of trouble in school.

Instead of sounding angry, Mrs. Blackwood sounded concerned. She asked Dad if there was anything stressful happening at home that would explain the brothers acting out in such a way.

When they got home, Dad looked nothing short of defeated.

"Is it the divorce?" he asked, his voice wavering. "Is that why you guys keep doing bad things? To get my attention? Please, just talk to me. Tell me how you're feeling."

"Dad," Jason tried, even though Elliot shot him a look to be quiet. "Please, you have to believe us. We didn't put those bugs in our projects. We swear! It was the—"

"No more lies!" Dad yelled, which made them jump. Dad never yelled.

"You blamed the mirror on some monster. Don't even think of doing

that this time. You're both grounded for the rest of the week. No computer. No video games. You'll redo your replicas for Mrs. Blackwood, and you will kindly ensure that *these* ones are empty."

With that, Dad stormed off to the basement, where he'd been repairing the stairs. Elliot looked at Jason.

"You were right," Elliot said, apologetic. "We didn't get rid of it after all."

Jason was having a hard time not bursting into tears. "We need

to come up with a better plan this time," he croaked.

Elliot nodded. "Or it's never going to stop."

# #7
# THE PLAN

The brothers sat up together into the night in Elliot's room, discussing what to do about the creature in the fireplace. Elliot agreed to let Jason sleep over since the chimney ran directly behind the wall in Jason's room.

"We could light the fire again," Elliot offered. "And just never let it go out."

"That wouldn't work," Jason said. "Dad wouldn't let us keep a fire running all the time. If he did, where would we get enough wood? What would we do when the weather warmed up? Who would get up at night to keep the fire going?"

"*Okay.*" Elliot frowned and crossed his arms. "I get the point. What's *your* genius idea, then?"

Jason thought for a moment, biting his lip. "The creature only comes out when Dad's not around to see it," he said. "If we could just

prepare ourselves for the next time we're home alone, we might be able to catch it. Trap it. Then we could show Dad when he got home, and he'd believe us."

"How would we do that?" Elliot asked. "What do we have that's big enough to hold it? And how would we capture it in the first place?"

"I don't know yet," Jason said, frustrated and suddenly tired of feeling afraid of the creature.

They were dealing with so many things in their lives right now. They

didn't deserve to have to worry that some horrific monster was going to get them into more trouble every single day.

"We're going to figure it out, though. We're not going to let this thing get the best of us."

"Whatever," Elliot said. He turned the lamp off and pulled the covers over his head. "We'll sleep on it and regroup in the morning."

"Wait," Jason whined, still sitting up in the dark. "We need to figure this out before we go to sleep!"

Elliot didn't answer. Jason knew he couldn't be asleep yet.

"Hey, Elliot," he whispered. No answer. "What did you mean a few days ago, when you said that I've been acting different lately? And you told me to stop lying to you."

Jason heard Elliot turn over in the bed, away from him.

"You told me everything would be fine," he mumbled after a moment. "When Mom and Dad started arguing more. You told me there was nothing to worry about. And

then you didn't act surprised when it turned out there was."

Jason took a few breaths, not expecting that answer. He had forgotten about that. He'd just hated seeing Elliot look so worried, would have said anything to make his brother feel better.

"I'm sorry," he said in a weak voice, but Elliot didn't answer.

Jason got up and left Elliot's bedroom. His own room was just as dark and somehow colder than his brother's. But Jason wanted to be

alone, even if the chimney *was* on the other side of the wall.

Had he done something awful by telling Elliot everything would be fine with their parents? Even when he'd started to realize that it probably wouldn't?

He must have, if that was the reason his brother had started acting mad at him all the time.

Jason got into bed, burrowed beneath the covers, and fell asleep. He dreamed that he heard the creature scratching the wall.

In the dream, the scratching got louder and louder, until little pieces of the wall started to fall away. "That's impossible!" Jason tried to cry as he watched, but to his horror, he was unable to move or speak.

The frantic scratching continued. Suddenly, a huge chunk of the wall opened up, revealing the black metal tube of the chimney. Standing there, with her arm looped around the chimney to hold herself up, was Jason's mother.

"Jason!" she wailed.

"Why haven't you called me yet to tell me about your new house? It's so big in here. It took me so long to find you!"

That's when Jason saw that something was wrong with her hands. They were as big as dinner plates, and green, with long, clawed fingers, just like the creature.

"Don't be scared, Jason," his mother cried. She reached for him, the long, green fingers trembling as they stretched forward. "You and Elliot are my entire world!"

Jason gasped as he sat up in bed, awake, covered in sweat from the nightmare.

"I know what to do," he said to his empty room. His heart pounded as the morning sun filtered in through the blinds. "I know how to catch the creature."

# #8 GIVE IT BACK

Jason sat at the foot of the stairs as Dad put on his coat.

"I'll be gone for about an hour," Dad said.

"I just need to go to the bank for a quick meeting, and then stop for more paint. You and your brother be good. If anything like the mirror happens again, we're going to have a serious talk."

Jason's stomach fluttered. He hoped the creature wouldn't do anything awful while Dad was away. If it tried, Jason hoped that he'd be ready.

"Bye, Dad," he said much louder than he needed to. He wanted to be sure the creature heard him. "See you in an hour."

Dad gave a tight-lipped smile and closed the door. Jason went to the window and waited until he saw his dad's truck move down the driveway and sped out of sight.

He turned to face the house, going almost right to the living room. Dad had done a great job of fixing the room up since they'd first moved in.

The dust was gone, the floor was newly sanded and polished, and new wallpaper had been put up to cover the old.

The big, new rug on the floor had something on it, Jason noticed as he approached the fireplace. There were little gray piles of . . . soot.

Jason stopped, his eyes widening as he took in the sight.

All around the sprinklings of ash, he was able to make out footprints that tracked their way over the rug, behind the couch. They went all the way to a big shelf that contained numerous trinkets and framed photos of Jason and Elliot.

The creature had been out again, without him knowing. It could have easily ruined his plan.

Jason looked at the shelf, uneasy. When he saw what was missing, he felt like he'd been punched in the stomach.

A small statue of a glass horse, with one leg in the air, was gone. Jason knew for a fact it'd been there, and that the creature had taken it.

"Okay," he said out loud, turning to face the empty room. "I give up. That glass horse was my mom's, and she's not here anymore. If you destroyed it, it would break Dad's heart. Not to mention my brother, Elliot's, and mine too. Please just give it back."

As he spoke, Jason realized something that chilled his blood.

While there were ashy tracks of soot leading up to the shelf, there weren't any little footprints leading *away* from it.

The creature had never returned to the fireplace.

Jason turned around and looked up to the top of the massive shelf, and couldn't help but scream.

The creature was sitting on top of it. It reached down with a long, spindly arm wriggling its outstretched claws. In its other hand was Mom's glass horse.

"Give it back!" Jason bellowed at the monster, with a ferocity that he hoped would startle it into listening.

But the creature hissed and jumped down from the shelf. It skittered across the floor, dragging the glass horse behind it.

Jason dashed ahead and stood in front of the fireplace. He blocked the creature from being able to jump back inside.

"There's no way I'm letting you escape," Jason said. "Especially with my mom's horse."

Without breaking eye contact with the creature, Jason reached behind him to grab a fire poker. Dad had used it to jostle the wood around while it was burning.

He held the poker up, pointing it threateningly at the creature.

"Unless you want to become a creature kebab," Jason muttered, taking a few steps forward.

"You'll drop that horse and leave this house forever. If you don't, I'll never stop coming for you until you do."

89

To his immense relief, the creature stepped backward as though it were nervous. *It's working!* he thought, taking a step forward, backing the monster into the corner.

The green thing with the big hands and snarling mouth gnashed its teeth. But it still looked too scared to try and dash past him to make it to the fireplace.

Soon, Jason had backed the creature against the trunk where they kept spare blankets for the couch. The trunk was open, and the shivering creature jumped inside to hide beneath the blankets.

Within a second, the top of the trunk came crashing down from behind. It locked with a *click* as Elliot stood up from where he'd been hiding since before Dad had left the house.

"I can't believe it worked!" Elliot cheered. He started laughing, the

first real smile Jason had seen from his brother since the day they moved into the new house.

"I can," Jason answered, lowering the fire poker. "Because we did it together."

"How'd you know the creature would be out of the fireplace?" Elliot asked as they sat before the locked trunk. All sorts of racket were coming from inside. "Or that it would take Mom's horse?"

"I didn't," Jason said, shivering at the memory. "I thought I'd have to lure it out, but it had already crawled over to the shelf by then. It

must have snuck out after we hid you behind the trunk, when Dad first told us that he'd be leaving soon."

*It had been an unexpected kink in the plan,* Jason thought. But in the end, it had worked out in their favor after all.

"I'm just glad everything went okay." Elliot's smile faded suddenly. "What about Mom's horse? It's inside the trunk, with that awful thing!"

Jason looked at the trunk. His excitement over capturing the

creature quickly faded into dismay. "Darn it. We just have to hope that it doesn't get broken while we're waiting for Dad to get back."

"Of course it will," Elliot said sadly. "The creature knows how much we want it. And I'm sure it's less than happy to be trapped inside a trunk. It's going to want revenge."

Jason bit his lip. Dad had only been gone for ten minutes. He still wouldn't be back for nearly an hour. Who knew what the creature would do to the horse in the meantime?

"We could get it back," Jason realized, "if we opened the trunk and grabbed it."

Was he actually considering doing such a thing?

"No way!" Elliot exclaimed. "The creature will escape and get away! And this will all have been for nothing."

A lump formed in his throat. He thought about how his nightmare had led him to realize that he and Elliot could only succeed in catching the creature if they worked together.

The creature had heard them arguing that first day it came out of the fireplace. It had never expected them to combine forces.

He knew the Mom in his nightmare hadn't been real. But she *had* reminded him that no matter how far away he and Elliot were, she'd always love them and want to know everything about their lives.

He couldn't let that glass horse be destroyed.

"The horse was Mom's favorite," Jason said. "She gave it to us when

98

she moved because she wanted us to think of her when we looked at it. Even more than she wanted to keep it for herself."

Elliot nodded slowly. "So what you're saying, is . . ."

"Mom's horse is more important than Dad believing us about the mirror and the insects," Jason said. "What if we released the creature in the woods and told it to never come back? I bet it'd listen. It was pretty scared of me when I was holding that fire poker."

Elliot thought it over. Inside the trunk, the creature screeched and rattled around.

"Okay." Elliot stood up, then pulled his brother up by the hand. "Let's do it, then."

Jason grabbed the fire poker. With his other hand, he clutched his side of the trunk by one of the thick, leather handles. Elliot took the handle on the other side.

Together, they lifted the heavy trunk off the floor.

"Hurry," Jason said.

They made their way out the back door and toward the forest beyond the oversized yard. "We have to get as far away from the house as possible and still get back before Dad gets home."

"Let's just hope it runs away." Elliot didn't sound too sure. "There's a solid chance it'll just run straight back into the house. Or it might eat us."

"If it goes back into the fireplace," Jason promised, desperate not to lose the feeling of control, "we'll tell

Dad that we heard a bird get stuck. So he's forced to run the chimney cleaner through it and discover the truth."

They walked into the forest until they could no longer see their house.

"This is as good of a place as any," Elliot said, setting down his side of the trunk with a sigh. "Let's open it."

# #10
# WHAT'S INSIDE?

"Promise me something," Jason said. "Before we open the trunk."

"What?" Elliot asked with mild impatience, clearly nervous about the possibilities of what might happen once they let the creature out. "Is now really the time?"

From inside the trunk, the creature scratched and wailed. "Yes," Jason said. "I think now is the only time."

"What is it?" Elliot brushed a piece of hair off his sweaty forehead.

"Promise me that no matter what happens when we open this trunk, we figure out how to get through it together." With every word, Jason felt a little bit lighter and less afraid.

"No more being mad at each other for things that are out of our control. If there's anything the creature taught me, it's that we're capable of getting through anything if we stick together."

Jason cleared his throat, trying not to cry as he continued. "I didn't mean to lie to you about Mom and Dad, Elliot, I swear. I just . . ."

"I know," Elliot said, surprising Jason with a hug. "I was just mad. At everything, and everyone. It's not fair that Mom had to move far away, and we had to come here . . ."

Jason noticed that the creature had quieted once they had hugged. Elliot seemed to notice too. They stared at the trunk as though expecting some sort of trick.

"You're right," Jason said. "None of it is fair. But we'll adjust, like Dad said. And he'll adjust, too, eventually. Probably we just need to be patient. I think we're all going to have to work together at that. He's been so sad lately."

"He has," Elliot agreed. "It'll get better now without all the fighting, though."

"And now that there isn't a horrifying creature living in our fireplace," Jason added. The boys laughed together.

In the distance, a crow squawked. It reminded them of what they had originally come to do.

"Go ahead then, I guess," Jason said, raising the fire poker like it was a baseball bat. "I'm ready."

"Okay," Elliot said. He pushed his sleeves up and crouched over the trunk.

"In three . . . two . . . one . . ."

Elliot unlocked the trunk and it clicked open. He lifted the lid and jumped backwards with a little yelp.

Jason waited for the creature to come out, but it was still hiding.

"Maybe it's scared," he suggested in a low voice. "Kick the side of the trunk or something."

Elliot took a step and peeked into the trunk. "No way," he said in disbelief. "That isn't possible."

Without lowering the fire poker, Jason took a step forward. "Is the horse okay?" he asked, worried. "Did it break?"

"See for yourself," Elliot said, his face unreadable.

When Jason got close enough to see inside the trunk, he gasped and dropped the poker.

Sitting on top of the blankets was Mom's glass horse, unbroken. Elliot grabbed it carefully, cradling it against his chest as they looked in the trunk with shocked stares.